Songs in the Key of Death

J.G. Faherty

LVP
PUBLICATIONS

"Songs in the Key of Death is a collection of edgy, stirring poems from the author of such well-known books as Ragman and The Wakening. I was delighted to learn that JG Faherty is expanding his horizons into poetry, and the result is a fascinating compilation of dark enchantments. Highly recommended!" —*Jeani Rector, Editor of The Horror Zine*

"I love the way JG Faherty's extraordinary poetry collection plays with language, form, and emotion. These pieces are by turns frightening, melancholy, disturbing, smart, and darkly witty. Songs in the Key of Death is a hit!" —*Lisa Morton, six-time Bram Stoker Award® winner*

"I really enjoyed this collection. The poems are philosophical and eerie, sometimes brutal and disturbing, with a lot of sharp edges and concise choices of language and imagery." - *Erinn Kemper, horror and weird fiction author whose stories have appeared in Tor.com, Black Static, Chiral Mad, Prism, Cemetery Dance Magazine, Dark Discoveries, and other markets*

Lycan Valley Press Publications
1625 E 72nd St STE 700 PMB 132
Tacoma, Washington 98404
United States of America

Printed in the United States of America

ISBN: 978-1-64562-002-0

Songs in the Key of Death

Contents

Introduction

Funny. I've written introductions to other peoples' books before, but not my own. So, first of all, let's get something out of the way. I never considered myself a 'poet.' Until now, if you'd asked me, I'd have said I'm a writer of short stories, novellas, and novels. And yes, now and then a bit of poetry when the idea hit me for something.

But over time, I started to realize that I'd written more poems than I realized, but I'd never submitted most of them anywhere. Mostly because I didn't think anyone would publish them; after all, I wasn't a big-name poet in the horror genre. But a few years ago, right before the pandemic, I had a couple published and people said they liked them. So when the lockdown arrived in 2020 and 2021, I had more free time than usual and decided I would seriously try my hand at writing poems. And I had fun with it!

Between those and the ones I'd already written, it turned out there were enough for a collection. Who'd have guessed?

However, I didn't want to just have a mish-mosh of stuff. I wanted a kind of feel to it. The original title for the book was going to be *Anatomies, Anomalies, and Anemones*, because a lot of the pieces involved mad scientists, body horror, weirdness, and sea creatures. But the more I thought about it, anemones is only 1 kind of animal, and there weren't actually any anemones in the poems! Then I started thinking about how songs are often poetry that is put to music, and all my poems involved death in some way, so then it became *Songs in the Key of Death*. Some word play on Stevie Wonder's *Songs in the Key of Life*, obviously. But then, I did that with my second short story collection, too. (*Houses of the Unholy*; thank you, Led Zeppelin!)

I'm glad MJae Sydney at Lycan Valley Press Publications agreed with me about the title, I'd have hated to try and come up with something else, because just like when I switched to *Songs in the Key of Death*, it would've meant adjusting the table of contents and substituting some different poems to fit the new theme.

So that's the story of how my first poetry collection came to be. I hope you enjoy reading it!

—JG Faherty
May 2023

Frankenstein Spurned

Flesh, sinew, blood
Copper, steel, bronze
Combine, transform
Something dead, something not

Life, love, vibrant
Cold, hard, sterile
Solder, suture
Something old, something new

Tissue, red, white
Metal, gray, cold
Muscles, motors
Clockwork wheels, tendon strands

Gleaming, sloughing
Gaping holes, spinning gears
Movement, arms, legs
Turning cogs, rigid rods

Alive, awake
Open eyes, open mouth
Bend, flex, breathing
Flow, spark, pumping fluids

Aware, aghast
Screaming eyes, crying mouth
Pain, terror, tears
Anger, hate, me

Begging, pleading
Put me back, put me down
Knife, stabbing, quiet
Dead, gone again

Promised, lying
Start over, hating her
Punish, hurt, revenge
Because she loved another

Natural Selection

I kill them when I see them.
I have to; they're evil, horrible creatures.
Hairy legs, poison fangs,
Multi-orbed alien features.

They hide within the shadows,
Lurking, waiting, pouncing on their prey.
Dissolving from the inside,
All who come their way.

Cold and calculating,
No emotions, fear, or sympathy
Death on eight legs
They remain my morbid fantasy.

No light undertaking,
Their dried husks litter my collection
The ultimate predator,
Carrying out my natural selection

Evolution

Waves swell and crash against the shore.
Rough and rising.
I watch from the terrace, alone now.
A lonely sentinel.
The ocean, always a cradle of life.
It continues to be; another chapter.

The pulsing womb gives birth, always has.
Never ending.
Animals, plants, microscopic at first.
But they grow.
Gills to lungs, fins to feet.
Metamorphosis, evolution, mutation.

A cycle to all things, always so clear.
But we were wrong.
Cycles within cycles, some long, some short.
Facts unrecorded.
No predicting this cycle, no clues, we said.
Lack of geologic evidence.

Some knew, though. Visionaries. Long ago.
Inscriptions, drawings.
We chose not to listen, see, believe.

Foolish and modern.
That time is past, we believe now.
Does it matter? Did it ever?

Footprints on the beach this morning.
Erased now.
All things are erased. By the sea.
By time itself.
The waves are stronger now than when I woke.
Birth is always a violent thing.

It won't be long now. I wait, I watch.
They are coming.
The next generation to inherit the Earth.
The next cycle.
Not the final one; never a final one.
But it will be the final one for us.

Happy Anniversary

Skeleton hands rise up from the grave
Ripe with mold, gloved in clotted earth
Yellowed finger bones waver, blind worms.
Clutch the screaming woman by the hair

Companions in lies, tables turned
A bottle of wine spills red, blood red
Pale imitation of a lover and friend
A fatal toast to the deed contrived

Twelve months past but never forgotten
A lich haunted by time and memory
Canyons carved in fleshy landscapes
Revenge a blue plum staring blankly

Teeth speak with gnawing phrases
The sound of deceit finally silenced
Greedy hands, no longer empty,
Return to darkness unmarked, unending

Husband and wife, parted, united
Ever after, a reality discovered
Whispered words only she can hear
Happy Anniversary, my love.

Speak Not The Words

Beyond our ken lies the black doorway,
the bridge to the otherworlds.
There wait the ancient ones, the true gods:
Cthulhu, Yog-Sothoth, and Nyogtha.
Blocked from our world for countless aeons,
they send forth their minions.
The ones who skulk in the gutters and shadows,
infesting the our world.
Orifices gnash in rabid anticipation,
Waiting for the day when the book is found.

Read not from the wicked Necronomicon,
the words within hold the power.
To summon those who dwell in darkness
and let the Old Ones walk again.
Destroyers of sanity, devourers of souls,
corruptors of the human race.
To call them forth is to open the gates of Hell,
and bring death to Mankind.
In the eternal darkness of their horrific triumph,
They will pillage and defile the Earth once more.

A Shipwrecked Holiday

Warm waves lapping on the sandy shores
White clouds floating in a sky of blue
Sun beating down, setting my skin all aglow
And broiling bodies lined up in several rows

I stroll the island in my solitude
Stomach rumbling like an angry lion
Warm sand 'tween my toes, hungry smells in my
    nose
I'm hoping soon it will be supper time

I know I've only got today
To prepare these bodies before they spoil
Without a fire, without a knife
But if I don't eat I'll surely lose my life

And so I watch the bloated corpses change
Shades of blue and green and gray
Flesh softening so nice, soon I won't be
    thinking twice
Once survivor's guilt finally fades away

Hammer Time

They live in my brain
I feel them; each day, all the time
Squirming, sliding, moving between and
    through
Fingers, worms, tendrils, roots, vines
Meaningless names for the things in my head
The things no one can see
No one but me

As long as I can remember
Eating my thoughts, devouring me
Nibbling, gnawing, chewing away ideas
Pieces, bits, crumbs, gobbets, chunks
All the things that make me what I am
The things no one can see
No one but me

Draining me more and more
I can hear them, laughing, talking
Whispers, shadows, no one believes me
Crazy, nuts, psycho, mad, weird
But they'll believe me soon, when I'm open
Then everyone will see
The things in me

The Jesus Orchid

Perennial, ancient, epiphyte
Spider network rooting on trees
On flesh
Curative, restorative, deadly
Returns health, returns life
And more
Photosynthesis, digestion
Dormant stage, feeding stage
Parasitic
Single blossom, crimson
Tendrils waiting prey
Attaching
Color changing, green to red
Permanent fixture
Symbiosis
Chemicals, enzymes, toxins
Protection from disease
Instant healing
Other names, other uses
Resurrection Orchid
Zombies
Personality changes
No predicting, no prevention
Often evil

Spores, seeds, embryos
Pollination, population
Plague

Jelly

Lying on the sand
Soft, deflated
Clear blobs of jelly
Filled with death
Radiating lines
So faint, so tiny
Filaments and canals
Tentacles like string
Nemocysts
Stinging, burning
Gloves required
Handle carefully
Still armed
Press between bread
Peanut butter
Wax paper
Time for school
No one steals my lunch
After today

Extreme Makeover

Open the box, snuggle against the pillow.
The toe sits, neat, on pink satin
Such a pretty thing.
Tiny nail painted fire-engine red.
Stroke it, revel in the feel.
Skin on skin; cool on warm.
Living on dead.
Remember the taste of it
Bland pale flesh, salty gamey tang.
Rolling on the tongue.
No more now.
Flesh dries, essence fades away
Like bubblegum chewed for hours.
Well and truly dead.
Just the way it should be.

Almost midnight. No one home.
Mamma's room is dark. Empty.
Inside the closet, the altar waits.
Mamma always keeps it ready.
Light the candles, make the square.
Red, white, black, yellow.
North, south, east, west.
Incense, so familiar, pungent.

Wormwood for death, rose for life.
Toe in the center, balanced
A miniature tower of flesh.
The taste of rum, sugar and fire.
Repeat the prayer, call the gods.
Loco, Grand Bois, Damballah-Wedo.
Ask them, beg them, entreat them.
Whole again, healed, purified.
Toe on stump, flesh melding.
A shriveled mummy brought to life.
Brown and wrinkled
Like its neighbors.
All dead, all alive.
No time to marvel.
Naked now, patterns traced.
Rum on skin, breasts and belly.
Speak the words.
Call the darkness.
Samedi! LaCroix! Legba!
Make the offer they require.
Blood and pain, sacrifice.
Seven times the prayer.
And then the garden shears.
One toe left, one pink giant.
No time to think.
The loas of Death hunger
And laugh.
Agony explodes, too much.
Don't pass out!
Scream. Screaming is good.

Catch the toe, tumbling.
Blood. Dripping. Flames.
Candles smoke and sizzle.
Black sparks, anti-stars.
Squeeze, wring, repeat.
All the blood is theirs.
Dying flesh twitching.
Then still.
Done for now. Time to clean.
Rum and wax, seal the wound.
Thank the gods, death and healing.
Earth, Sky, Sea, Underworld.
Stumble to bed.

Big toes hurt the worst.
But only so far.
The real worst is yet to come.
Many months of pain.
Piece by piece. Small to large.
Killing. Reanimating.
Becoming something new.
Something better. Stronger.
Immortal.
Time for sleep.
But first just a taste
Like old pennies on the tongue.
Close the box.
Hands shaking.
They know they're next.

Purgatory

Suicide is not painless
And it only changes one thing
The final place of your misery
I hated my life and my death
But it was too late to change anything
To stop the bleeding

So many cuts
I did it to end my pain
The pain was only the beginning
No darkness for me
No white at the end of the tunnel
Only gray light, gray life

All the people, all around me
Gray faces, but not lifeless
Sad. Angry. Depressed.
We're all here now
The ones who could not cope
Miserable, wretched pieces of shit

Denied happiness for eternity
Locked in shells of despair
I hate them. I hate God.

I hate me
I always did
Now I always will

From Darkness Born

Te Po rules the night, *Te Kore* owns the dark,
  from deep within the well of chaos
Give birth to *Rangi* and *Papa*, whose embrace
  delivers those who are the source from which
  all things come
Creating the creators on a cosmic scale
Or perhaps producing the egg of life and
  destruction, from which *Ta'aroa* sprang to
  make the sky and earth and then fill them
  with blessings and curses only blood
  sacrifices can appease
Different gods, different paths, but nothing
  changes
Ao and Po, man and woman, day and night
Do they create that which we know, or was it
  Tangaloa, ruler of the sea, who shaped
  humans from maggots and provided hearts
  and souls?
Lono, Maui, and *Oro* look down at *Tu*, who
  brings weapons to bear. *Tane, Pele,* and
  Tawhiri mollify, appease.
While *Kamapua* ruts with the women, polluting
  the blood of man even further.

Mana fills the world, good and evil, beautiful
and terrible, hot and cold. In all things, from
rocks to man.

It is the power of life and death.

The power of magic.

With magic come the canons of the world.

Spiritual restriction, implied prohibition.

Tapu.

The golden rules for all to follow. Penalties
contained within. Sickness. Bad fortune.
Death.

Mortality is everywhere, darker than dark, more
powerful than life. The end of life, but never
an end to itself.

Death lies wrapped in kawakawa leaves, a
funeral rite across the eons. The spirits'
journey to the ancestral lands is long and
dark and the dead skins are silent.

Tapu demands it.

The *karakia* of the living matter not;
desanctification solves nothing.

Travelers bring *kawe mate; rangatiras* and *toas*
tattoo lines of life and death on sullied flesh.

The pantheon of creation and legend arises from
the dark and descends into it, swirling,
revolving, whirling.

Chaos eternal.

Tapu unending.

Islands of death.

The Tumor

A growth discovered in the brain.
Or stomach, or lung, or liver. It doesn't matter.
The tumor is there. Remove it.
An odd-looking thing. Yellow. Pulsing.
Lock it away for further examination.
Call in the experts. This is new.
Open the jar. Now there are two.
Fantastic! Astounding! What good luck.
Papers, fame, names in journals.
Grants and funds and equipment.
Look closer. Movement. What is it—
No! Soaking in, absorbing.
Memories gone, samples gone.
Months pass, life goes on.
Until the weakness, the tests.
The results are back.
A growth discovered in the brain.
Or stomach, or lung, or liver. It doesn't matter.
The tumor is there.
Remove it.

We May Never Know

I am not crazy.
They were here. The grays.
They came for me in the night.
Paralyzed, helpless, terrified.
They didn't care.
They took me with them.
Experimented on me.
Probes, electrodes, machines.
So much pain.
But I remained awake.
I saw everything.
Their faces, no expressions.
Emotionless beings.
Cold, so cold.
Their ship. Their hands.
Reptilian, amphibian.
Not alone.
Not me, not us.
Other subjects.
Other races out there.
All captured by the grays.
Mutilated, tortured.
And then released.
I don't know why.

I need to know. Help me.
Believe me.
Things in my head.
I feel them.
Xrays. Ultrasounds.
Find them. Remove them.
Help me.
I can't sleep.
Dreams. Memories.
Voices in my head.
Make them go away.
Your pills don't work.
Your words don't help.
Find them. Cut them out.
If you don't, I will.
I will.
I swear I will.

A Song Of The Sea

The gentle shush of passing waves
Lapping against the hull
Provides the steady beat
Leaping fish deliver percussive emphasis
While random whales sing arias
Evening breezes harmonize
Passing through the lines
The ocean's tune, once beautiful
Becomes familiar after so long
Then one night an interlude
A distant melody so new
Like nothing ever heard before
So beautiful in simplicity
It brings the eyes to tears
The heart breaks open in melancholy
Sylvan whispers, distant harps
Voices sweet and sorrowful
Bring images of grass so green
And meadows starred with flowers
Through days and nights the song grows
stronger
A beacon in the dark
Until islands appear and sailors cheer
Lost at sea no more

Upon the rocks the singers wait
Naked maidens in a pair
As lovely as any have ever seen
Crooning songs of no compare
Visit us, stay with us, be happy here
Wine and cheese, bread and meat
And pleasures of the flesh
With promises of such delight
The ship is guided forward
Until too late discovery
Of treachery and lies
Rocks that shatter hull and keel
And with them flesh and bone
The singers descend with teeth and claws
Sharp as any knives
To eat the flesh of those they lured
To feed their hungry tribe

iFuture

iKidneys failing. iHeart weak. iLungs gasping.
iDying now.
iDoctors no help. iHospital too expensive.
iFading fast.
iFriends gone. iGraves. iShips.
iAlone forever.
iMeds useless. iOrgans outdated.
iStore out of stock.
iWeb searches. iPages empty. iBills piling.
iBrain crazy.
iJobs non-existent. iInsurance gone.
iBroke again.
iStreets dark. iCitizens helpless.
iDesperate to live.
iFeds coming. iLaws broken. iJail waiting.
iCell dark. iMeds free. iParts waiting.
iCured.

Visitors ~ Part I

Something is here.
Upstairs. Creeping. Creaking.
Moving on tiny feet.
In the attic. In the walls.
Whispering, giggling.
Peeking through holes.
Stalking us, day and night.
Following our movements.
Waiting when we come home.
Leaving things for us.
Broken dolls, headless mice.
Scurrying in dark.
Gone before we see them.
Their words mean nothing.
Gibberish. Alien.
But angry, so angry.
You can feel it.
No one believes us.
We have no proof.
They disappear if people come.
Silent. Waiting. Watching.
Hiding somewhere.
Each night, there are more.
A constant pattering

Of feet and voices.
We should leave.
We know that.
But this is our home.
We will fight.
We are ready.
Why are they laughing

The Dentist

It eats me up inside
This rage
Overpowers me, takes control
A secret beast
Makes me hurt them, cause them pain

They don't know when it will happen
But I know
When I hold the tools once more
Sharp, pointed
My hands become instruments of torture

They want to scream, to shout
To cry
I don't stop; I go deeper
Deeper still
I smile behind my mask

Their blood is my joy, my goal
I want to laugh
I am the bringer of their pain
I hate them
Their vile, rotten mouths offend me

Rhymes With Blood

Flood, blood pours out, rivers flowing from
    wounds
Thud, before blood, bodies falling to the floor
Crud, when blood dries, crusting fingers and
    nails
Mud, blood on earth, thickening and hardening
Scud, run from blood, escape the storm that
    ensues
Spud, don't eat blood, yet the hunger's always
    there
Dud, give no blood, failure in the modern age
Cud, vomit blood, a scene played out again
Stud, brings forth blood, crushing through skull
    and flesh
Bud, blood brother, holds the body or knife

No more words, need more, more blood
Everything is blood, everyone is blood
Play in blood, bathe in blood
Life is blood, good is blood
Blood is blood is blood is blood
Blood blood blood blood blood blood blood
Blood blood blood blood blood blood blood
Bloodbloodbloodbloodbloodbloodblood

Groundhog Day In Hell

In horror's lair we found ourselves
Naked, lost, abandoned; memories erased
In darkness lying on the ground
Injured, cold, and bleeding; awareness gone
In terror we did cry for help
Screaming, shouts of fear; presence known
In desperation we did clutch
Blinded, reaching out; groping hands

Streaming tears and heaving breasts
Bodies packed in forlorn embraces
No consoling, no brave fronts
Just empty souls and murmurs
Time passing, unfelt, unseen
Hands of clocks, all unmoving

Minutes, hours, days uncounted
Hunger, thirst, cold asserted
Not death, then, but something else
Human, bodies whole, alive
Where then, why, how
Questions unanswered, lingering

In starvation bodies fading, falling

Songs in the Key of Death

Dying, cold, painful; withering away
In black of night branching out
Exploring, seeking; escape routes
In weakness wandering, lost again
Endless, far, hopeless; emptiness
In final breaths and final steps
Collapsing, done, finished; giving up

Gasping lungs, fluttering hearts
The end rapidly approaching
No bravery, no heroics left
Just resignation and despair
Blackness comes, and with it peace
Then we waken in this place again

The Oldest Profession

Galaxies and solar systems rotate, swirling and
    expanding.
Universes form, grow, and die.
Life emerges from a countless number of seas, evolves,
    becomes extinct.
Matter, energy, radiation, solar winds, it all comes from
    me, and returns to me.
You could say I am the alpha mother, the creator.
But there is a price to pay for everything.
Matter forms and energy is needed.
You cannot live without dying; you cannot grow without
    losing something of yourself.
I collect those payments; they're due to me.
The oldest profession?
Yes, it is, on a scale you cannot imagine.
I am the God-whore.

Penetration Hurts

Penetration hurts, in more ways than one.
That's the lesson I teach curious johns.
Like the guy who showed up yesterday.
He dropped two thousand dollars on the bed
Said he wanted something new.
Those words are magic to my ears.

He loved it when I used all three orifices on him
But changed his tune when my appendages
    appeared
Said I was a freak, he didn't want nothin' in his
    rear
They're all the same, enjoy the giving
Then run and hide when it comes to receiving
Not that their feelings matter much to me

He struggled, they all do, but in the end
I'm stronger, faster, and more experienced.
In two weeks he'll wake up with a big surprise
When he finds out what something new really
    means
Hope he likes being a mommy
Who's the freak now?

Seven Billion Skins

Seven billion, give or take
Black, white, yellow, brown
Tall, short, fat, thin
Covered in skin
All the same, each one
Underneath
Just a different cover
A different skin
Decoration, wrapping paper
Hiding identical gifts
Organs and flesh and blood
Men, women, children
Thinking, living, breathing
Race, religion, politics
None of it matters
Seven billion skins
And I want to peel them all

A Tennessee Alien Invasion

They arrived silently, at night.
No one heard them, no one saw.
One day, they were just here.
Hundreds of them.
Appearing out of nowhere.
Horrible creatures. Aliens.
Tentacles and beaks and nasty bug eyes.
It started on Friday night.
By Sunday, it was over.
Elmer shot the first one.
Then everyone started.
They tried to fight back.
At least, people say they did.
Some folks think they came in peace.
Said they spoke about galactic harmony.
Not that it mattered.
Not once we found out the truth.
Aliens taste damn good.
Now we're all waiting.
For the next batch to arrive.

Mind Fleas

Feel them burrow into your brain
Digging, scraping, chewing
Hear their thoughts inside your head
Urging, pushing, ordering
They want you to do cruel things
Hurtful, harmful, evil
They're never quiet, never sleep
Watching, waiting, begging
How long before you can't hold out
Crying, pleading, screaming
There's only so much a man can take
Relenting, caving, yielding
Follow their orders, do as they say
Stalking, following, attacking
Bring the bodies home for them
Eating, feasting, devouring
Try to explain, no one believes
Bullets, pain, blood
Dying, you realize the truth
Spreading, infecting, transmitting

Housebound

I'm so lonely, I could die.
I have nothing. No one.
Just a dark emptiness of the soul
To go with my dark and empty house,
I watch people come and go outside.
Their daily lives filled with fun.
With laughter and love. With each other.
While I have no one.
No one to talk to, to share thoughts with.
No one to hold my hand.
I cannot leave, my condition doesn't allow it.
I can watch them, the lucky ones,
But sometimes it just hurts too much.
Watching them only makes me feel worse
Drives daggers into my being
Jealousy, depression, anger
Sometimes it makes me rage.
I fly from room to room, shouting, ranting.
Flinging things from shelves
Until I am exhausted.
Then, spent and drained and weak
I fall back into my pit of despair.
Helpless to do anything except remember
While the world cycles around and around.

Passing days, passing months.
Until the light returns and I wake once more.
Then the cycle starts again.
Go to the windows. Stare outside.
Wait for the next family to move in.
So I can haunt them too.

Love Is

Love is:
>   Blood on a knife
>   Screams in the night
>   Terror-filled eyes

Love is:
>   A punctured lung
>   A severed spine
>   A missing tongue

Love is:
>   Stalking the prey
>   Gutting and carving
>   Bathing in red

Love is:
>   Victims in cages
>   Pleas for mercy
>   Shackles and chains

Love is:
>   The touch of cold steel
>   The burn of hot oil
>   The crunch of broken bone

Love is:

       The final gasp of air
       A clouding of the eyes
       Bowels releasing

Love is:

       Death in all its glory
       Victims piled high
       Mounds of rotting flesh

Love is:

       Scrapbook pictures
       Newspaper clippings
       The good old days

The Man In The Alley

Insidious
Lurking, secretive, corrupting
Always on the edge,
in the shadows

Stealthy
Creeping, stalking, prowling
Hidden from sight,
silent and deadly

Dangerous
Watching, violent, angry
Armed and primed,
a living weapon

Calculating
Devious, shrewd, cunning
Two steps ahead,
strategic planning

Methodical
Violation, mutilation, penetration
Patterns followed,
rules broken

Pathological
Accurate, surgical, precise
Clean and meticulous,
nothing wasted

Visionary
Genius, intellectual, master
Always a step ahead,
outwitting enemies

Invulnerable
Unstoppable, powerful, invincible
Force of nature,
never failing

Unencumbered
Free, liberated, released
On the loose,
Behind you

Nothing Changes

A transition with unexpected results
Loss and bereavement nonexistent
Pain, sorrow, darkness unfound
The tunnel and light nothing but lies
Just another place

Through the door nothing changes
Featureless, plain, rather dull
A gray mirror of myself
Just another space

The others are shadows, whispers
Moving, breathing, staring
An absence of interaction
Just another race

All the same, my gray clones
Featureless, plain, rather dull
People without meaning
Just another face

The Downer

My soul is dark cesspool
From which I never rise
I wallow in endless misery
Surrounded by my blight
All of my own making
I spread my despair everywhere
Corrupting and afflicting
A disease of the heart
Staining the pristine
Scarring the perfect
The sickness inside me
Is a constant virulent companion
A malady with no cure
A disorder of the human essence
Something to abhor
My soul is dark cesspool
From which I never rise
I spread despair everywhere
A foul, fetid deadly chi
All of my own making
My choice
Life is good

Why They Should Teach Latin

The day they rose up was a bad one for mankind
For so long they'd been waiting
Dormant, hiding, resting, healing
Until someone fool uttered the fateful words
Opened the gates, broke the bindings
Released them back into our world
Terrible things, monsters beyond ken
Maws that swallowed ships
Hands that squeezed the life from buildings
Cities trampled underfoot
Sacrifices demanded, blood and flesh taken
Bodies raped, breeding stock created
Weapons were useless against otherworldly
    magic
Some tried to find the answer, cast the spells
They failed in ways too awful to recount
Their screams lingering in the air
Long after their bodies became pulp
In the disaster and ruins of civilization
No one noticed that I was spared
How was I supposed to know the book was real
It was just an accident, I didn't believe
But I'm not telling them that

Jacob

Curled in a ball, mattress hard and unyielding.
Straight jacket binding tight. Tight as my jaw.
Speaking through clenched teeth hurts.
But not as much as what's inside me.
A ghost shouldn't hurt, but it does. So much.
I tell her, but she doesn't believe.
The doctors never do. They will.
She asks about possession. Humoring me.
I suppose she's right. I am possessed.
By Jacob. Everything I did, his fault.
He forced me. Needles in my mind. Stabbing.
I tried to resist. Couldn't. The pain, too much.
Who is Jacob? I know the answer. He's told me.
Ancient. And angry. Always so angry.
A leper. Spurned by Jesus. Denied a cure.
My jaw hurts more than ever. My face twists.
The anger is building as he, as we, remember.
The men. Stoning him to death. But he didn't
    die.
His spirit remained, fueled by hate.
Moving from person to person, making them do
    things.
Terrible things. Evil things. Like me.
I can't go on. I know what I did. So awful.

She urges me. McKenzie. My latest doctor.

Red dreams, I tell her. Full of pain.

Drool sprays from my mouth as I spit out the words.

Thousands of years, forcing people against their will.

People like me. Try to refuse. We all do. No use.

Razor claws carve your brain. Fire in your guts.

Only one way to ease the agony. Give in.

Kill them. Tear the flesh, eat the pieces.

Innocents. Me, them. Not my hands, my teeth. His.

Blood, so much blood. Taste in my mouth all the time.

Every day, another body. Twenty. Thirty.

I stopped counting. Jacob chooses them. Tells me.

Stab them. Take them home. Chop chop eat the pieces.

Make the pain go away, just for a few hours.

Over and over, no peace, until they catch you.

Only then will he leave, only then.

McKenzie frowns as I relax, my muscles limp.

I have time to wonder if my smile confuses her.

Then she screams. Now she knows. Now she feels.

The sudden blinding agony in her skull.

The voice, evil liquid fire in her brain.

Telling her what to do, urging her with knives.

Her shout tears from her throat. She won't.

But she will. They always do.
Now she believes. The words are Jacob's.
The guards rush in, just as he wanted.
They are not prepared. For her. For him.
Blood everywhere. Parts on the floor.
Her face buried in a man's stomach, chewing.
I remember what she is feeling, experiencing.
Pink and red hole, burrow deeper. Jacob's voice.
Laughter, insane, howling with joy.
Twenty thousand years.
Twenty thousand more.
I cry. For me. For her.
While Jacob keeps eating.

The Artist

Beauty is only skin deep.
I believe that. Under the envelope of flesh,
   everyone looks the same. Red, pink, white.
   Wet. Strings and strands.
Removing the skin is the great equalizer.
Peeling back the layer of falsehood.

That is my ultimate work, my masterpiece.
Showing the world the truth. Opening their eyes
   to what really matters. Equality. Uniformity.
   Parity.
No one is better than anyone else. Why can't
   they see?
Red, yellow, black, white, Jew, Catholic,
   Muslim.

Without flesh, what is the difference? Nothing.
I have to prove it. My gallery is the world and I
   paint on the human canvas. My knives are my
   brushes, each stroke genius.
DaVinci, Picasso, Matisse, Michelangelo,
   Warhol.
They all tried to change the world, but none of
   them had my vision.

I will do what no one has ever accomplished.
I will truly make the world a better place. A
    where unity rules and our children live in
    peace and happiness.
So please stop screaming.
Great art always requires sacrifice.

Studies In Anatomy

A single feather, plucked from the body of a
    dead robin.
Gentle, intricate, amazing in its complexity.
A life time of fascination and examination
    kindled.
A thirst to know, to learn, to discover.
Magnifying glasses and microscopes.

Afternoons spent on sidewalks, observing.
Ants, beetles, slugs, worms. Alive. Dead.
A moth with no wings, stolen from a lamp at
    night.
Powdery, fragile, yet with the power of flight.
A thousand tiny scale, a thousand veins.

The urge to compare, to test, to see.
Legs, wings, antennae, carapaces, thoraxes.
One after another, caught, broken, pinned.
Puzzle pieces, see how they fit together
Questions unanswered, yearnings unsatisfied.

A tiny finger, clipped from the body of a frog.
Muscles, vessels, tendons. Bone and sinew.
So different, so much more to learn.

Organs, skin, flesh. Eyes, teeth, tongue.
Systems within systems, a living, breathing
    factory.

Needles, batteries, wires. Experiments
    conducted.
Sacrifices in the name of science. The joy of
    learning.
A howling cat, impaled on a broken stick.
Warm, bleeding, fighting. Nothing like the
    others.
Yet so alike. Never giving up, yearning to
    survive.

Eyes glazing over at the moment of passing.
A soul leaving? Or just the absence of oxygen?
More reading, more studying. What is life. What
    is death.
No one knows, no one understands. No one
    agrees.
Science is the key, the path to follow

The neighbor's dog, lying on a table.
Open, pumping, beating. Everything familiar.
All the same on the inside. Cats, dogs, squirrels,
    mice.
Jars filled. Hearts, eyes, brains, livers, kidneys.
Different in size, identical in form and function.

Frustration growing. No answers found.
    Nothing learned.
Something missing. Something wrong. Craving
    truth.
A single breast, carved from a pretty
    streetwalker.
Soft and unique. Distinct from all others.
Every part special, singular, exceptional.
    Diversity.

Finally on the right path. People are not
    animals.
No predicting. Some fight, some submit without
    a struggle.
New jars, new collections. New studies for a
    life's work.
Watching the lights go out, still no answers.
Not yet. But with enough subjects... one day.

The Tavern Of The Dead

In the Tavern of the Dead
The drinks are always free
But you still must pay a price
Time is the coin of this establishment
And your account is endless
Drink up, drink up
Your glass is never empty
Only your soul is depleted
By the relentless monotony
Everyone knows your name
And you know theirs
Your companions in Purgatory
Sit down, place your order
You're never getting up again
Death slides you a tepid beer
Or whiskey, or tequila, or wine
Your choices are limitless
Next to you a fat man asks what time the game
    starts
Just like he does every day
You hate everyone and wish you could die
Then you remember you already have

Plastic Surgeon

Scalpel, needle, gauze
Implants, sutures, suction tube
The tools of my trade

A new face, a new chest
Or nose, or eyes, or legs
Each one a fresh canvas for me

Enhancement, enlargement
Reduction, removal
I don't change, I create

They always say beauty
Is in the beholder's eye
So Behold! I shout.

But they're all blind
To my works of beauty
They called me a monster

Deformed, hideous
Grotesque parodies of life
Who are they to judge

J.G. Flaherty

No false beauty
Only my creations
Made in their maker's image

Mrs Panagopoulos

She watches from the window at the top of the
    house
Every day I see her
Just a face
Never smiling, never speaking
Simply staring
Mornings when I leave, evenings when I return
Always there, watching
Just a face
Never moving, never changing
Gazing out
How long she's been there, I couldn't say
Longer than I have
Just a face
Never sleeping, never reading
Looking down
Winter, spring, fall, summer, year after year
Always in her same cloths
Never aging, never graying
Just a face
Just a face

The Telepath

Thoughts crowding in, so many, so loud
Everywhere, every time, everyplace
Every little thought from every dirty head
A thousand conversations, her, him, them
Nasty intruders, filthy brains filled with poison
Sex and lies, fears and secrets
Lust and hatred, terrible loathing

The last one my own, loathing everyone
All the same, horrid words and pictures
Dirty parts, dirty deeds, sickening
See the truth, no one sees it but me
Nothing hidden, nothing sacred
Murder and rape, theft and death
Violence and greed coins of the realm

Drenched in blood and body fluids
Vice rules, kindness drools, no one wins
Money fuels need, need fuels desire
No stopping them, no shutting them off
Must keep listening, have to
The silence is so much worse
Because then I hear my own thoughts.

Reflections

My reflection stares at me
Through the clear water of the lake
It smiles. Is it happy to see me?
Am I happy to see it?
I don't know. I can't tell.
I don't feel anything.
That should make me happy.
Maybe that's why other me is smiling.
The pain is gone.
My body, my soul, nothing there.
All the negative emotions swept away.
Exactly what I wanted.
Smiles can mean so many things.
Happy to see me.
Happy to see me go.
Who is leaving who?
Who is smiling?
Which one of us is real?
And which one is drowning?

Baby Holly

She sits on the shelf, all porcelain beauty
White as snow, white as bone
Delicate as sugar glass
Every detail crafted to perfection
Red lips, blush circles, brushed hair
A dress of the finest silk and shoes of leather
I like to smile at her
My little doll, my Holly
Sometimes I bring her to other rooms
To have tea, or watch the world go by
We don't like the sunshine
Her skin is too fair, like mine
When I read, she looks over my shoulder
Her eyes the bluest of blues
Her fingernails the blackest of blacks
My little doll, my Holly
Henry keeps telling me I have to let her go
But I don't. I can't. She's mine.
The perfect child
Not like that screaming, bloody thing he put
   inside me
Never again

Zombie Blues

It wasn't supposed to be like this.
Not for the world, not for me.
A virus. That's all it took to change everything.
The dead rising like mutant corn stalks.
Only we couldn't put them down.
Because they were like us. Alive. Aware.
No rotting corpses starving for human flesh.
Just people. Ordinary people. Like you and me.
Only the recent dead carried the bug.
The unembalmed corpses in morgues and
    hospital beds.
But that was enough to produce a new society.
We were terrified at first, the living.
People screamed as loved ones awoke and
    returned.
Hysterical nurses fled as pronounced bodies sat
    up.
But humans adapt, and fear can only last so long.
Paradigms shifted, a new order came to be.
Society evolved to meet the latest wrinkle in the
    fabric.
Healthcare, employment, the burial industry.
Patterns developed and mankind moved forward.

Cancers and other diseases no longer evoked
    fear.
Kill the patient; he or she woke up cured.
Helmets became all the rage for drivers.
Head trauma, brain damage the only sure killers.
Religions slunk off into the night amid global
    laughter.
And people like me got a new lease on life.
Death sentences lifted by a simple microscopic
    organism.
When my day arrived, I gladly threw it all away.
The pills with their radioisotopes.
The IV bags with their chemical compounds.
One simple injection. Lights out for Henry.
And tomorrow back to work without a care.
That's how it was going to be. My future bright.
Now look at me. Stuck in this chair. Paralyzed.
It wasn't supposed to be like this.
Not for the world, not for me.
The world got a goddamn miracle.
I got hit by a car on the way to the hospital.
On the day I forgot my helmet.

Troll Hunter

Stalking the prey is half the fun
Hours spent in unnatural habitats
Searching for spoor, tracks, signs of passing
Evidence left behind, a trail to follow
Back to the den, the dark sanctuary
A hunter needs to be wary at all times
Trolls are unpredictable forces of nature
Sometimes solitary, sometimes living in groups
Masters of disguise, shadow lurkers
They carve and claw at things they don't
    understand
Violence rages inside them, seeking outlets
The human world is not a place for them
They seek to destroy what others build
Existing only to bring sorrow and pain
Their lives are meaningless without hate
Venom drips from their tongues and fingers
When I find them, I put them out of their misery
And everyone else's as well
But I have to wonder
What did they do before computers?

The Animalcules Shall Inherit The Earth

In the darkest depths of the ocean
Where light never reaches
In the farthest reaches of space
Where warmth is just an illusion
At the tops of the highest mountains
And in the cracks of ancient rocks
They exist
Wonders of nature, hiding from sight
Life forms so alien they shouldn't exist
Body chemistries abnormal and wrong
Consuming the impossible, the
    incomprehensible
Poisons, sulfur, petroleum, copper, manganese
Even electricity and nuclear waste
They thrive
Unstoppable miniature life machines
Reproducing, repeating, dividing
Capitalizing on anything and everything
Or lying dormant for millennia, waiting
For just the right moment to emerge
The right host, the perfect substrate
They win

Killing Me Softly

He doesn't use knives or acid or guns
Or other instruments of torture

He doesn't lock me in metal cage
Or chain me to a wall
Leave me naked and covered in filth
Deny me water, make me foul myself

He doesn't pull out my nails
Put hot pokers in my eyes

Or even yank my teeth one by one
He doesn't rape me, violate me
Abuse me with his fists or his words
He doesn't leave me alone for days at a time

He doesn't beat my flesh to a pulp
Break my bones, starve my body

He doesn't kill my family or friends
What he does is so much worse
He loves me, day after day
And he never stops
Even when I beg him to

Ghosts In The Walls

There are ghosts in the walls of this house
If you listen close, you can hear them
The floor board that creak at night
The strange rattle or bump in the attic
The footsteps in the hall just as you fall asleep

They are not imagination, they are real
Every house is different, but the same
Haunted by those that came before you
Some come from death, some from sadness
Some from a longing to remain in this world

Spirits are like homing pigeons
Returning to the place they loved
Or the place they hated the most
Ghosts are just people without form
Angry, happy, lonely, sad, wandering, adrift

They are everywhere they used to be
No one leaves, no one moves on
There are ghosts in the walls of your house
If you listen, you can hear them
Someday, you will be one of them

A Conspiracy Rant

What ancient mysteries lie 'neath the seas?
Civilizations only rumored to exist.
Miracles of engineering and medicine
    undiscovered.
People like us, or perhaps not.
Aliens, mermen, soldiers, builders, seers.
Living lives in the times before time.
So many tales handed down, legends and stories.
So many clues buried by layers of antiquity.
We don't understand what we unearth.
We don't believe the ones who do.
Who are the crazy ones? The theorists?
Or the scientists with their facts predetermined?
Tsoukalos, Von Danekin, Riley Martin.
Laugh at them if you will.
But what will you do if they're right?
Ancient drawings depicting flight
Mysterious spaceships in the night
Massive boulders at impossible heights
Your explanations carry no more weight
Than those of the crazies you choose to hate

Under The Big Top

Bells and whistles, calliope music, merry-go-
rounds and Ferris wheels.
What fun! What joy!
Children laughing. Hurrying parents from booth
to booth, ride to ride.
Excited! Shouting!
The sounds are loud, the lights are bright. A
thousand odors fight for attention.
Sensory overload!
Candied applies, corn dogs, cotton candy,
lemonade, funnel cakes, fried Oreos.
The tastes! The smells!
Teenagers try to beat carnies at fixed games,
wasting hard-earned dollars.
Darts! Rings! Balls!
The tall figure stands in the midway, dressed in
the garish colors of fall.
Yellows! Reds! Oranges!
His tent waits, its excitement masked by the
gusting October breeze.
Rippling! Quivering!
The autumn man places a stovepipe hat on his
narrow head and eyes the growing crowd.
Ready! Set!

He raises a megaphone to worm lips, his other
    spindly arm stretched wide.
Welcome to the show!
"Ladies and gentlemen! Come and see what
    waits inside the Big Top tonight.
Hurry! Hurry!
Fire breathing dragons. Two-headed lions.
    Giants with arms of steel. A flying god.
Step up! Step up!"
Excited patrons stream inside, eager to see.
    They laugh and jostle as oddities emerge.
Creatures! Monsters!
Laughter turns to screams as dragons and beasts
    pluck away tender prizes.
Clawing! Rending!
Blood sprays in all directions, body parts fall to
    the filthy straw.
Death! Destruction!
Panicked throngs swarm for exits, but there are
    none, no escape to be found.
Trapped! Surrounded!
Quetzalcoatl winds through the masses,
    swallowing virgins raw and whole.
Sacrifices! Offerings!
An ogre clubs a man to death while new widows
    and children crouch beneath bleachers.
Cowering! Hiding!
The autumn man joins his minions, his
    impossible smile expanding across his face.
Wider! Wider!

His huge mouth opens, ear to ear, exposing
multiple rows of jagged fangs.
Deadly! Poisoned!
At the Carnival of Fear, the midnight show is
just beginning.
Endless. Hungry.

A Winter Storm

Snow falling, a winter wonderland
Everything white, everything silent
I watch through the window as nature lays down
    a blanket
And the world goes to sleep
The birds are roosting safely
The squirrels are snug in their nests
No cars, no people, nothing to mar the beautiful
    serenity
That stretches on and on
I marvel at the frozen landscape
Death hiding behind a white mask
How hardy is the wildlife to survive such
    extremes
Where I could not live
I continue to gaze as the sun descends
White to gray to charcoal
The clouds hide the sunset in horizon wide
    shadows
The coming of night
Snow continues to fall, deeper and deeper
The blizzard of the century
Up to the window of my car now, and no end in
    sight

Burying everything
I wonder when they will find my body

My Girl

Her lips are soft as rose petals
Pink as a baby's blush
Her eyes are gray like a cloudy day
But they look at me with love
Her hair is soft as the finest silk
And black as midnight sky
She's everything I've ever wanted
And I'm proud to call her mine
Her legs are long oh so shapely
Her breasts are twin perfection
Her nose is small and delicate
A button on a doll
Her body fits me perfectly
When I hold her in my arms
Every piece of her belongs to me
And I'll never give them back

Harvester Of Eyes

I have a job to do, just like you. Don't judge me.
I come for the things inside you. Parts and
    pieces.
Your organs belong to me. You just don't know
    it.
But you will. I show up when you least expect it.
Not in the hospital, when you are too sick to
    move.
Not at the scene of an accident, as you lay dying.
Not in your bed at home, with hospice
    attendants.
Not even in when that hooker drugs you in the
    hotel.
When you least expect it.
After you die.

If that makes you laugh, it shouldn't.
You don't know all the answers, the real truth.
You don't just die when you die. That's my
    secret.
The soul lives on, the mind continues thinking.
No heaven, no hell, no reincarnation.
Just bodies in the ground, cogitating. Talking.

Lots of conversations and theorizing down
    there.
Until I show up. Then the talking stops.
Everyone goes silent.
They fear me.

Because what I do causes them pain.
I come for what is mine. The parts. The pieces.
Livers, kidneys, lungs, hearts, spleens.
I take them, I need them. To replace my own.
That's how I go on and on and on and on.
And the eyes. The eyes are the most important.
So I can see. The other-life is a dark, dark place.
A hard place, where things rot away too quickly.
I don't want to die.
So I steal.

A little here, a little there. From him, from her.
It's my job, I don't have a choice. I have to.
Why else would I be here? It's what I am. What I
    do.
I rebuild myself from the parts of others
Remake myself constantly. That's my purpose.
To bring pain and suffering to the dead.
To make them feel again, if only for a moment
To make them quiver and cry in their dirt beds
Your turn will come
I promise

Against My Will

Sick, sick, sicker
Illness in the mind, the body
Leave me alone, leave me alone
Stay away
Keep your hands off me

Doctors tell me everything that's wrong
Chemical imbalances, organs failing
Liver, heart, lungs, brain
Shut up! I don't want to know
Why are they doing this to me?

Chemicals, cures, surgeons, knives
Radiation in my blood
Tell me nothing; tell me lies
None of it real, just dreams
Stay out of my head

In the chair, on the table
People talking, no one listens to me
I know, I know, I know
Why have they done this to me?
Just let me go to sleep

An Ode To Death

Death is a skeleton on a black horse
Or a man with a gun
Or a needle in the arm
Death is anyone, anything at all
Me, you, a neighbor
The car coming at you
Death is sure, death is random
An accident, an illness
Old age, a broken stair
Death is everywhere around us
On the plane, in your food
In the air, in the wires
Death comes in the day and night
By phone, on TV
In the newspapers
Death stalks and prowls
Hidden and open
Quiet and loud
Death is a goddamn motherfucking
Piece of shit

Old Habits Die Hard

The old man stands on the front porch of the
retirement home.
Chill October air burns aged lungs with the first
frost of winter and a hint of wood smoke.
Memories awaken, simpler times when houses
all had fireplaces instead of electric heaters
with fake logs.
Gleeful cries echo from the street in reaction to
candy dropped into paper bags, pillow cases,
and plastic pumpkins.
Simpler times, safer times. People trusted
people in those days.
Seventy years. Has it really been that long? It
should be just yesterday.
The night he discovered there was more to
Halloween than just candy. 70 pages turned
back.
All the excitement, the costumes, the sack heavy
with coins and apples. So different then.
"Hey mister! Trick or treat!" Three pint-sized
cartoon characters running down the path.
Reverie broken, time line reinstated.
Orange bags clamor for attention. Eager bodies
dance in place. Too soon, not yet.

A bony, liver-spotted hand lifts up. His own.
How sad, how wrong.

Candies fall into waiting receptacles. "Have a
good night." They run off, quest still
incomplete.

The book of memories opens again, demanding
to be read.

So different then. Everyone knew everyone.
People paid attention, noticed things.

Like a small child disappearing.

Five years in a juvenile home. Bad times, hard
times.

But he'd learned from his mistake. Be careful.
Watch. Learn. Plan.

He'd played the part of good citizen upon
release. Reformed. Repented.

And then moved away at twenty-one to start
over.

That's when the fun began.

In those days, fun got measured in months and
years. Not minutes. Not like now.

Another change, another difference. And not for
the better.

Forced to wait. But that he could still do. Wait.
Something he was good at.

He'd practiced enough.

And now the waiting was over. The familiar
pressure back after so long.

With it came other feelings. Lightheadedness. A
rapid thrumming in his chest.

Not good for the old ticker. But what did it matter?

Eight hours. Eight hours to be young again.

He wouldn't need that long.

More voices approaching. His heart jumping and jiving in its cell. One caged beast inside another.

Sudden darts of pain across his ribs. Angina. Not good. Time running out.

Then again, not unexpected. The little blue pill had always symbolized the end.

One last hurrah for old times' sake.

Two figures skipping towards him, a black cat and a little vampire. Perfect.

"Come inside. I've got a big bowl of candy and cups of hot apple cider."

They enter, no fear of an old man in place filled with old men. Old men are nice.

Old men are safe and have candy.

The screen door closes, followed by its heavy wooden partner.

The screams begin before he finishes turning the lock.

The show is in full swing when he enters the kitchen.

Kitty cat on the floor, yowling in fear. One quick slash of the knife and her cries turn into a bubbling sigh.

She slips to the floor, topples over, joins the other bodies on the cheap tile.

Vampire tries to run, but blood is like ice. He
    slides and glides, feet dancing beneath him.
He falls to his hands and knees, and then it's
    time.
Time to be young, time moving backwards, time
    running out.
Groin pulsing in time to the hammer blows of
    pain behind his ribs.
What will last longer, the Viagra or his heart?
The vampire cries, like all the others, unaware
    he's the last of his kind.
The final hurrah.
There will be one more death tonight.
But what a way to go.

Can You See The Real Me

Stripping away the false pretenses that hide the
    truth
Removing the masks, the disguises, the
    costumes
I reveal myself to the world
I no longer care if they are ready to see me
The time has come to throw open the windows
To show myself as I really am
No more need for shells, for appearance's sake
For excuses, for blending in, for being like the
    others
The truth shall set me free
There is pain but I am ready for it, I embrace it
Birth, rebirth, the phoenix rising from the ashes
The delivery of the new me
I don't expect people to understand, not all of
    them
A few perhaps, enlightened bulbs scattered in
    the dark
Seeing beyond pretenses
The camera documents everything, my release,
    my screams
Revealing what lies beneath, under the lying
    flesh
That which is really me

Mr Fred

Mr. Fred, Mr. Fred
I woke up screaming in my bed
Three weeks ago, in the middle of the night
I remember now, everything he did, everything I
    felt
The pain, the humiliation, the terror

Mr. Fred, Mr. Fred
His name keeps bouncing in my head
Memories buried so deep, locked away
Even when the shrinks probed and questioned
    me
Were you ever molested, neglected, abandoned

Mr. Fred, Mr. Fred
I thought the truth was what I said
Of course not, those memories would never fade
It's just me who's off, who lost his cool
Bad behavior, poor decisions, I took
    responsibility

Mr. Fred, Mr. Fred
I knifed a man, killed him dead
But not the man who raped me when I was eight

The one whose face I see every night now
Leering, staring, laughing, watching me go by

Mr. Fred, Mr. Fred
Past his house the roadway led
Every neighborhood has a man like Fred
    Pembruller
A fellow who sits on his porch and watches the
    world
Someone you wouldn't pay attention to

Mr. Fred, Mr. Fred
Into his house I was led
"I need your help, Johnny," the trick he used
I suspected nothing, things were different then
People trusted each other, kids listened to
    adults

Mr. Fred, Mr. Fred
A darkened room lay ahead
I turned around and saw the gun pointing at me
Big as a cannon, the black hole staring into my
    eyes
"Not a word or I'll put a bullet in your skull"

Mr. Fred, Mr. Fred
"Turn around, legs spread"
He stripped me naked, bent me over a chair
I didn't scream, not when his moist hands
    touched me
Not when I felt the first stabbing pain

Mr. Fred, Mr. Fred
Agony repeated
Three times he took me, my jaw clenched tight
Tears running down my cheeks, I watched them
    fall
When it was over, he gave me a cloth to clean up
    with

Mr. Fred, Mr. Fred
White cotton turned to red
"Put your clothes on and get out," he growled at
    me
"Don't tell a soul how I made you a man"
He waved the gun, his threat all too real

Mr. Fred, Mr. Fred
Not a word I said
Fear had its claws deep in my soul
People would call me a queer, a faggot
For the things I let him do to me

Mr. Fred, Mr. Fred
A normal life I led
On the outside, I pretended nothing was wrong
My wounds healed, I went to school, I played
    sports
But I never went near his house again, not for a
    year

Mr. Fred, Mr. Fred
He made me live in dread
Then he moved away, and a weight lifted from
    my soul
Months and years passed and he faded from my
    memory
Leaving behind an anger that I didn't know the
    source of

Mr. Fred, Mr. Fred
He's back inside my head
I don't know what triggered the memories, the
    dreams
Therapy, perhaps; or the news of my mother's
    death
My time served, a new start on life thanks to her
    will

Mr. Fred, Mr. Fred
Time to plan ahead
An apartment, a car, a computer, and a name
Fred Pembruller, not so many of those in the
    country
Weed out the ones too young, only 89 left to
    visit

Mr. Fred, Mr. Fred
Time to make them dead
I started last night in Davenport, Mississippi
I was careful; I learned a lot in prison

Like how to have fun while leaving no clues

Mr. Fred, Mr. Fred
I watched him while he bled
It wasn't the right one, but that doesn't matter
Sooner or later I'll find him, and when I do
It's amazing what you can do with a broomstick

Mr. Fred, Mr. Fred
I'll see you in your bed

In Darkness Born

In darkness born of deep despair
I contemplate the unthinkable
My knives lie ready, shining and pristine
Waiting to carve through supple flesh
Plastic bands grip straining wrists and ankles
Pleading eyes stare at me through veils of tears
Bruises standing out like purple flowers
Painted on an alabaster canvas
I watch from my chair, my emotions churning
So easy to stand up, to select a blade
Begin tracing intricate designs of death
Action follows thought, I rise and move forward
The implements of my intention call to me
They are prepared to do their part
Slicing, carving, gouging, peeling, chopping
Turning one form of beauty into another
Easing the boiling turmoil in my soul
Satisfying this primitive desire
She grows frantic as I draw closer
Her naked chest rising and falling entrances me
I raise my hand, which suddenly holds a scalpel
I never noticed, too trapped in my dilemma
Tears create meandering streams on her cheeks
I feel matching rivers on my own face

She begs for mercy in whispered tones
Her screams long since reduced to moans
I can't help pausing, listening to them
So wrong, how could I end up like this
Betraying everything I believe in
Deep breaths, fight the urges
Reminding myself that I am the one in control
The master of what I choose to do
My hand grips tighter 'round the handle of the
    knife
In darkness born of deep despair
I contemplate the unthinkable
Letting this one live

A Modern Jesus

Miracles performed
Water to wine, bread multiplied
Feed the poor, heal the sick
Walk on water, part the seas
Spread the word of peace
Cure the blind, raise the dead
Talk of Heaven and redemption
Love thy neighbor as thyself
All sins can be forgiven
An end to war, bloodshed done
Extend the olive branch
Television demonstrations
For all the world to see
God's love for everyone
A world filled with harmony
Taken away in the night
Prodded, tested, sampled
Opened, tortured, drugged
This time he won't get free
Until all his secrets are known

Blood Red, Corpse White

The end is coming
Blood red and corpse white
I welcome it and dread it
I did what he asked, just as the others did
Pen and paper, so different
Others at the strange machine
Apologizing for things never done
No one will understand
Except him

"The confession will heal your soul"
I screamed: "My soul is fine"
Is, was. His fault. He did this to me
Put this evil inside me, made me see it
All he had to do was tell us
Send us back, set us free
We could have changed
I would have changed
He knows about time
It flexes, bends, breaks
Time is clay. Time is lava
"I cannot take chances"
I respect that, and hate him for it

He sobs and cries. Depressed savior
The knife shakes in his hand
He cries
He doesn't stop. One after the other
Killing the wrongs
Fixing the world

The others are gone now
Blood red and corpse white
He saved me for last. Confessed
A life time of watching, waiting
The visions eating his brain
All he wants is peace
His soul, the world
Still he cries
"There is none"

At the end, I despise his terrible faith
"The box could have been wrong
Not my future, not my path," I plead
Not me doing those things I haven't done"
"The box never lies. It cannot"
I watched him with the others
First the knife. The blood
Then the note. The mouth
Finally my turn now
The pain - sharp, cold
I can't scream. I taste paper
"Goodbye. It ends with you"
Words. Far away. I'm dying

Everything dark. I hear the box open
He screams. Like I did. Why?
The box?
Footsteps on stairs. Where is he going?
What did he see?
What is his future?

The Parasite

We are one, joined together in harmony
I touch you and you quiver with joy

My skin crawls in disgust, revulsion fills me

The bond between us is so magnificent

I want to die; I want this to end

I can't imagine a life without you

I want you gone; I hate this life

Your form fills me with happiness
I get lost just contemplating your beauty

I can only pray for this nightmare to end

When I feel you move, it is a communion of
   spirit

Your very existence repels me, I want to scream

Your flesh is soft, like rose petals in spring
I breathe your essence, apple and honey

You are a blight in the eyes of God

You are perfection personified, magnificent
You are the lowest of lows, vermin

The thought of losing you makes me weep
The thought of you dying makes me laugh

With our bodies joined, I am complete
I wish our symbiosis could go on forever

I dream of the day I am free of you
The day I finally hatch and fly away

The Collection

They line the shelves, boxed and jarred
My collection of oddities so rare
Things you never think of
A piece of slimy demon flesh
A lock of Hitler's hair
Fungus from a faery garden
Bones from an ice age bear

Everything here has a price
But nothing is for sale
My unexpected treasures
A pen that only writes in blood
The last known dragon scale
The antler from a unicorn
And of course a mermaid's tail

For so many years I've gathered
Things that should not be
All of them real
Fingernails from a lamia
Fruit from Adam's tree
A satyr's hoof preserved in oil
Houdini's magic key

My list of things is never ending
Pan's flute, Triton's spear
Manticore wings
The Eye of Ra
All of them are here
And all you need to do to own one
Is trade me that which you hold most dear

Visitors ~ Part II

Something is here
Downstairs. Stomping. Thumping.
Invading our territory.
Occupying the big spaces.
Talking, shouting
Giant monster things
Stalking us day and night
Setting traps for us
Trying to drive us away
We tried to appease them
Left them gifts and sacrifices
It did no good
Their cries frighten us
Their words mean nothing
Gibberish. Alien.
But angry, so angry.
They hate us
It took us so long
To build our numbers
Hiding in the shadows
Patient. Waiting. Watching.
Carving our weapons
Each night, we make more.
While we listen and learn.

They are foolish.
They should leave.
We will beat them.
This is our home.
We will fight.
We are ready.
To start the killing.

The Mermaid's Tail

I caught a fish that spoke to me
"Please don't kill me," was her plea
"Let me live, I'll fulfill your dreams."
This was no ordinary fish, it seems.

"What magic is this?" I did cry.
"I've been cursed," came its reply
"I was a mermaid, a princess too.
That's a secret, 'tween me and you."

Through the tangles of my net
She begged me, "You must keep me wet."
Her story she did for me regale
While swirling water with her tail

"An evil wizard became my enemy
And then he cast a spell on me
Took away my human half
Then cast me out with a laugh

Now it's likely that I'll die
Unless break the spell you dare to try."
"To break the spell, what would I do?"
"All I need is a kiss from you."

Kiss a fish? A repellent act.
Then I pondered a certain fact.
Gold and riches must await
The man who frees her from her fate.

Surely a reward she'd give
Food and money so my kin could live
So I touched our lips together
Very chaste, light as a feather

And watched in awe as change did she
Into a lovely woman from the sea
Golden hair and breasts divine
Azure eyes like jewels did shine

"You've saved me!" she cried out with glee
"Now cut this net and set me free."
I took my knife and grabbed the net
"Tell, me, what payment do I get?"

She shook her head and shed a tear
"You ask the question that I fear
All I had is forever gone
Stolen by he who did me wrong

Like you I find myself in need
Your payment is this one good deed"
I gazed at her, this creature fair
And thought about my cupboards bare

I contemplated, hard and long
To let her die would be so wrong
In the end I had to do what's right
That's why my family's eating well tonight

The Doctor

Whenever you're not feeling well
A house call he'll be making
He'll slither from beneath the bed
And make sure that you're not faking

He'll check your heart, your eyes and ears
While you quake and shake and shiver
He'll say, "Don't you fear, the Doctor's here,"
Before cutting out your liver

With bony hands and leering smile
He'll swing his needles and his knives
He'll hack and slice, chop and dice
While you fight to stay alive

Blood falls down and hits the ground
Creating puddles on the floor
While you scream and flop around
As he carves you up some more

So unless you want to meet this fate
Here is what you need to do
Eat right, stay warm, don't get sick
And the Doctor won't come visit you!

The Mushroom Garden

Bloodless, pale faces glow
like putrid toadstools,
surprised by the glare of the flashlights.
I saw them first. First arriver.
First with the sticky, slimy
taste of death on my tongue.
The first shall be last,
and the last shall be first,
the Good Book says. Why?
Why? He wouldn't say. Maybe
someday I'll know. Maybe
I'll never know. Maybe
no one will. Everything
by the book and yet
I did everything wrong.
Another prize at the end
of another maze. The house
next door. A quiet fellow.
I never thought about him.
Then open windows delivered
the smell of death. My Sally
always says I'm too nice.
"No good deed goes unpunished."
Christ, I've heard that

On the job and in the bedroom.
I wonder what Sally thinks now.
Who really gets punished?
When I went inside his home,
calling his name, a foul stench
choked me. There were no sounds,
no reply. Empty house. Clean.
Tidy. The porcelain sink gleamed.
But the basement door—the stink
greeted me halfway down.
In my mind, another death certificate
to fill out, another senseless ending.
What this time? Heart attack?
Broken neck? Bee sting?
A memory surfaced: an old man—
stroke, half-eaten by his cats.
Death is a lonely business. Doubly
so when you live by yourself.
Of course, he wasn't alone. I learned
death can blossom in flashlight's glow:
Bulging eyes. Scraps of paper sticking out
from silently screaming mouths.
So many of them: like a wet garden
of broad, white capped mushrooms.
Something moved and I turned
slow. Too slow.
A wrinkled face
rushed me. Screaming.
The glint of a knife.
Pain—my ribs. It's worse with every breath.

Then, the luminous white mushrooms
bursting wet and cold beneath me. Bloodless,
Their pale, putrid faces, glowing.
Welcoming me into the garden.

Stepping Out

Angie lies there sleeping, I wish her dead
Boredom fills me, excitement gone
Her beautiful face, I feel nothing for it
Married too long, ennui our daily pattern
We need a change, alteration of modalities
Romance rekindled, lust stoked to life
Something new; someone new
"I will fix this," my whispered promise
There is no choice, no going on this way
Bring back what we had, the way we felt
Before we grew jaded, before this rut
Return the spark, the feeling of new

No time is wasted, online searches are easy
Tonight will be different, new choices made
Someone interesting, someone intelligent
More than a body, more than Angie
This hole inside me, this empty place
Yearning to be filled, to be satisfied
Conversation, that is what I crave
A need for things, things my wife can't give
Love is strong, love is not always enough
Mental stimulation, the missing link
No infidelity, no breaking our bond

Truths were told, permissions granted

Stomach quivering, butterflies and rats
First date anxiety, feelings long forgotten
Importance not lost, this is for us both
Angie deserves better, not through the motions
A blind date the cure, an opposite chosen
Brunette not blonde, tall not short
Not a dancer, a teacher chosen
Breaking the pattern, going against type
The only hope for this, the only chance
Find the anti-Angie, awaken the sleeping me
Return me to life, bring back the man
Angie deserves that, deserves all of me

She arrives on time, a vision in red
Eyes sparkle in blue, skin glows pale
All heads turning, she glides through the room
Satisfaction fills me, a choice well done
Introductions made, flesh cool and soft
Conversation starts and stutters, a nervous pair
Wine is ordered, glasses sipped and sipped
     again
Worst fears brewing, guilt rears an ugly head
Is this wrong, is this the way to fix things
Can't back down, can't go home defeated
Another topic, how was your day
Her smile beams, funny you should ask

A piece of steak on my plate, a bloody fetus

My head nods as I chew, words fill the air
Incessant ramblings, inane chattering
The ceaseless barrage, the vapid stories
How is it possible, how can a head be empty
Thoughts like silver balls, bouncing to and fro
A verbal pinball game, changing without
    warning
A neon 'tilt' sign overhead, half-expected
Manicures and hair, television and celebrity
    gossip
Endless prattle, a litany of sameness
No different at all, despite careful selection
Simply Angie, Angie in a different shell

The verbal river pauses, for air or for a response
No way to tell, I nod and murmur something
Her smile flashes, see you understand and why
    couldn't
White noise again, thoughts of Angie return
Wrong so wrong, not what I wanted
Stuck with the same thing, no change at all
More wine poured, her smile turns tipsy
No need to get me drunk, we know where this is
    going
Fingers trace my arm, resignation wells up
The game must be played, only one possible
    ending
A job to do, a conclusion to be delivered
Hopeless and gray, my night unfolds

From the edge of the bed, watching her slowly
strip
Her self-absorption aids me, shields my softness
from her
Nothing new here, this narcissistic tendency
A term coined be me, The Paris Hilton
Syndrome
Angie didn't appreciate the name, didn't laugh
A bad case of it herself, superficial to the max
Now her twin is found, despite the planning
My sigh grates on my teeth, there will be no
change
The same old same old, going through the
motions
My hands slides down, the frustration building
Will it always be like this, what is the point
The hammer is waiting, cold steel too familiar

The thought hits out of nowhere, my body
frozen by it
I am the catalyst, the source of change must be
within
Break the cycle, assert force in a new direction
Determination a new variable, my attention
focuses on her
Lithe body and feline movements, sensual and
nude
Blessed silence, the greatest aphrodisiac
Excitement twitches in my lap, the hammer is
released

Bodies join on the bed, soft breasts caress flesh

Tongues dance and play, hands explore new
vistas

Passion grows stronger, begs for release

Strong hands pin her down, animal urges take
over

The night disappears, long gone before I finish
with her

Morning returns, sunshine and renewed zeal for
life

The girl is gone, her satisfaction evidenced by a
number left

Perhaps to be called again, perhaps never
needed

Energy radiates through me, batteries recharged

An answer so simple, an antidote found

Physical rather than mental, a change effected

A new ending written, unexpected but right

Senses renewed, basement stairs descended

Angie awaits, the ideas abounding within me

Bruised puffy eyes greet me, limbs pulling
against chains

Muffled screams ignored, the morning's tools
selected

So much to tell her, so much fun to be had

Freddy Johnson Misses The Rapture

Is there anybody out there?
I peer from behind a curtain of my own making.
Alone for too long, not long enough.
Fear still guides me, caution the mantra.
The memory fresh in my head.
Watching them disappear, just vanish.
Bright bursts of light and then nothing.
As if they never were here, never existed.
I don't want to be one of those.
No telling where they went, who took them.
So many gone, familiar faces missing.
This place is empty without them.
I was alone once before, until I found them.
Now I'm alone again, on a larger scale
I need to find others, I don't like alone.
But outside is where the bad things happen.

Is there anybody out there?
I watch, a constant vigil from my sanctuary.
I have no idea what I'm looking for.
Please don't take me, I don't want to leave.
No one hears me, my words are silent.
Unseen, unheard, unfound, unsafe.
I cannot stay here, I cannot leave.

Watching the emptiness, who is watching me?
Waiting for a sign, who is waiting for me?
Not what I wanted, not what I chose.
Who will be next, what is the order?
I wish something would move, show itself.
So long now, weeks, months, I don't know.
I am like a ghost, haunting nothing.
Is it over? Did they miss me, forget me?
I have to leave, I cannot move.

Is there anybody out there?

Ana

She comes to me in the night, answer to my
    prayers
My Goddess; where would I be without her
Perfection offered, challenge accepted
Out with the old, in with the new and improved
No place for self-hatred, not anymore
Not with the help of the Goddess
Bloated and disgusting, a fat, ugly creature
No more; the road to perfection awaits
Almost there, with her help and my sisters
Bones grinding against bedsprings, delicious
    pleasure
Prayers at night, say them together around the
    world

*I believe in Control, the force that brings order
    to my chaos.*
*I believe I am vile, worthless, and useless,
    unworthy of love.*
*I believe others would hate me if they could see
    the real me.*
I believe in perfection and the drive to attain it.
I believe in salvation through starvation.

I believe in the abnegation of the body and a life
of fasting.

Thin is perfect, thin is beauty, thin is the goal
Love waits, the other side of the mountain
Ana is that love, enough for all of us to share
Follow the rules, ascend to the promised land
Look but don't taste! Smell but don't touch!
Think, think, think about food and how to avoid
    it
Temptation is the devil, calories are the enemy
Punishment the answer, replace guilt with pain
Do not fail her, never that, never again
Thin at all costs, nothing else matters
Keep Ana happy, keep the dangers away

I believe in devotion to Ana and her sister Mia.
I believe she watches over me and keeps me in
    line.
I believe no one else matters but my Goddess.
I believe she is the only one who understands
    me.
I believe she protects me and all her children.
I believe she keeps me safe from those who
    would do me harm.

Losing weight is good, gaining weight is bad
Being thin is more important than being healthy
Ana's teachings, set in blood and flesh for all

Listen to the scale, ignore the family
Destructive words come from frowning faces
Not eating leads to success and power
Thin equals attractive, starvation equals joy
Buy small clothes, take diet pills, skip meals
All in the name of the one true Goddess
Ignore the haters, those who follow the wrong
    path
Ana protects, Ana saves, Ana punishes

I believe in Hell, because I live it every day.
I believe in a black and white world, with
    unbreakable laws.
I believe in losing weight to eliminate my sins of
    gluttony.
I believe in the power of thinness over negativity.
I believe in retribution against my enemies,
I believe in honoring Ana and making her
    proud.

In the darkness she arrives, thinner than the eye
    can see
A terrible beauty, that which we strive for
Tonight is a night for vengeance, for justice
She is the reckoning, come to defend her child
No more tubes, no more pills, no more doctors
Down the hall she glides, slipping through
    cracks

Screams, shouts, lessons taught to the
  blasphemers
Ana and Mia my true parents now, and forever
Quiet, peace, freedom; the last barriers torn
  down
Ana awaits, in her heaven without food or shame
I will honor her and make her proud

To the end of my life and beyond

Road Rage

Horns blaring songs of senseless anger and
   frustration
Mechanical elephants stampeding in a concrete
   jungle
Stampeding to nowhere, nothing moves in this
   place
Fists pound wheels and irate mouths shout
   virulent epithets
I see them all around me; I join them, all control
   lost
Time creeps forward, passes by, moves along
Able to do the one thing the traffic cannot
   accomplish
Not good, not good, I don't need this kind of
   trouble
Not today; warnings circle like starving vultures
New client, important to make a good
   impression
Can't be late, can't screw this up, gotta beat the
   competition
Fate is a damn bitch, something has to be done
A motorcycle breaks loose, flies past on the
   shoulder

Freedom! A bird among the earthbound,
    unfettered
Temptation rises; spread wings, soar down the
    highway
Two miles to the exit, five ticks of the minute
    hand
Problem solved, extra points for ingenuity and
    fast thinking
My hands grip the wheel but sirens freeze them
    in place
Flashing lights racing forward, alien spacecraft
    in my mirror
Police, ambulance, the shoulder their lane now
Something alive inside me, swimming frantic
    circles
Fear, that unwelcome visitor, come to play again
No escaping now, no leaving the formation
Tickets mean certain failure, a doomsday notice
Trapped in hell, a victim like all the others
A scream rises from me, unbidden, unstoppable
It draws no attention, lost in the surrounding
    din
The radio mocks me, a sudden breaking news
    story
My story, my assignment, completed by another
This will not end well; pink slip, termination
Sudden birdsong fills the car, unwelcome
    interruption
Innocuous tones producing chilling
    premonitions

They say a picture tells a thousand words
The one on my phone produced only five
My family is dead; murdered
Nothing left for me, my last hope gone
In my briefcase, salvation waits
The gun unused, the message undelivered
Now it will have its chance, a new message
    written
Gearshift into park, no change in forward
    motion
Metal cold against sweating flesh, hand
    trembling
The final sounds before the white light takes
    everything
Honking horns, shouting voices; road rage

True Love Never Dies

True love never dies
Vows exchanged, wedding night promises
Laughter and love forever, a long road together
Hills and valleys, obstacles to overcome
An acceptance of imperfection
Delivers the perfect relationship
Sailing the river of time, more than a river
A carnival ride, tricks and hidden doorways
Entering undiscovered countries, uncharted
    waters
Steeper hills, deeper valleys, more obstacles
Seeds sown in darkness, emotions sprouting
Vines and tendrils, creeping, insinuating
Taking over, overgrowing, covering
Crumbling old structures finally falling

True love never dies
Poisoned and rotting, shambling along
A creature in a funhouse mirror come to life
Trapped in the boat, riding with the ferryman
Styx is a river unending, Hades its home
Minutes are torture, days are agony
Words become daggers, rooms become cold
Beds grow barren, meals silent battlefields

Suffering and torment bring vivid dreams
Freedom, release, starting over again
Plotting, scheming, hidden behind fake smiles
Motions to go through, concealing the truth
Strategies equal hope, ideas become reality
Deeds carried out, secrets buried in deep graves

True love never dies
Memories become ghosts, haunting the living
Guilt tarnishes bright futures, stains new joys
Circles are revealed, impossible circumstances
Sounds, odors, shadows moving in the night
Voices whisper, dark pledges terrifying
Visits promised, familiar vows repeated
Cycle of emotion, love, hate, fear
Styx flows on, landscape different, destination
    unchanged
Sleep the new enemy, cold fingers caressing
Heartbeats stolen, sanity drained away
Constant companion, everywhere, every when
Acceptance becomes inevitable, destiny
    becomes doom
A knock on the door signals the ultimate truth

True love never dies
Even when you think it has

Show And Tell

In this bag there is a secret
One I'm not supposed to show
I stole it from my father
Who doesn't think I know
The thing that sits inside it
Is valuable and old
I heard him telling mommy
Its power is foretold
He said it was an amulet
A word I'd never heard
And that it's really dangerous
But that just seemed absurd
If it wasn't safe to have it
Mom would yell and shout
Like she did about his gun
And make him throw it out
I decided I should see it
So I snuck into his room
And opened up the velvet bag
While hiding in the gloom
It looked like crummy jewelry
Kind of junky, kind of cheap
But something whispered to me
That it was mine to keep

I put the chain around my neck
And then went back to bed
That night I had the strangest dream
Crazy pictures in my head
The stories that they showed me
About a boy who would be king
Who wore the mighty amulet
Instead of some old stinky ring
He led a massive army
That swept across the lands
And held the power of life and death
Within his own two hands
I woke with such excitement
What a story I had to tell
But when my parents saw me
Onto their knees they fell
They said I was their master
We worship you, behold!
And then they pledged allegiance
Said they'd do what they were told
That's what gave me this idea
Why not bring it in to school
And put it on in front you
To begin my eternal rule

Acknowledgements

As always, I want to start by dedicating this book to my wife, Andrea, who continues to suffer through all the time I spend at the computer putting thoughts into words. Despite not being a fan of horror or dark fiction, she continues to be my biggest supporter.

I also want to say thank you to my mom, Terry, who reads every one of my books and promotes me to all her friends.

Special thanks go to my beta readers/friends/best critics Rena, Brian, Lisa, Patrick, Chris, Jim, and Erinn.

And, of course, I have to give a shout out to MJae Sydney for turning this collection of poems into a reality and giving life to death (very Shelley-ian!), and all the people at Lycan Valley Press Publications who worked on it—without editors, designers, and artists, books would never see the light of day.

Finally, I want to say thank you to some people who don't even know they helped me, but it was their work as dark poets, publishers, and editors that made me think I could do this. So thank you, Kathryn Ptacek, Jeani Rector, and Rich Ristow for publishing some of my first poetry and Linda Addison, Lee Murray, Angela Yuriko Smith, Geneve Flynn, Christina Sng, Edgar Allan Poe, Michael Arnzen, Wrath James White, and Stephanie Wytovich.

Credits

- Natural Selection *(previously appeared in ScienceFictionFantasyHorror.com, 2005)*
- The Dentist *(Previously published in Wicked Karnival, 2006)*
- Against My Will *(previously appeared in The HorrorZine, 2013)*
- Blood Red, Corpse White *(previously appeared in Death in Common, 2010)*
- The Doctor *(previously appeared in The HorrorZine, 2013)*
- The Parasite *(previously appeared in Horror Writers Association Poetry Showcase Vol. IV, 2017)*
- The Mushroom Garden *(previously appeared in Death in Common, 2010)*
- Show & Tell *(previously appeared in The Horror Zine, 2013)*

About The Author

A life-long resident of New York's haunted Hudson Valley, JG Faherty is the author of 19 books and more than 85 short stories, and he's been a finalist for both the Bram Stoker Award (2x) and ITW Thriller Award. He writes adult and YA horror, science fiction, dark fantasy, and paranormal romance, and his works range from quiet, dark suspense to over-the-top comic gruesomeness. He is a frequent lecturer on horror and an instructor for local teen writing programs. He grew up enthralled with the horror movies and books of the 50s, 60s, 70s, and 80s, and as a child his favorite playground was a 17th-century cemetery, which many people feel explains a lot. His influences range from Mary Shelley (a distant relative!), Edgar Allan Poe, Jules Verne, and Tales from the Crypt comics to Stephen King, Karl Edward Wagner, and Alan Dean Foster. You can follow him at https://www.twitter.com/jgfaherty, https://www.facebook.com/jgfaherty, https://www.instragram.com/jgfaherty, and www.jgfaherty.com.

www.ingramcontent.com/pod-product-compliance
Lightning Source LLC
Chambersburg PA
CBHW020227120726
47903CB00008B/2579

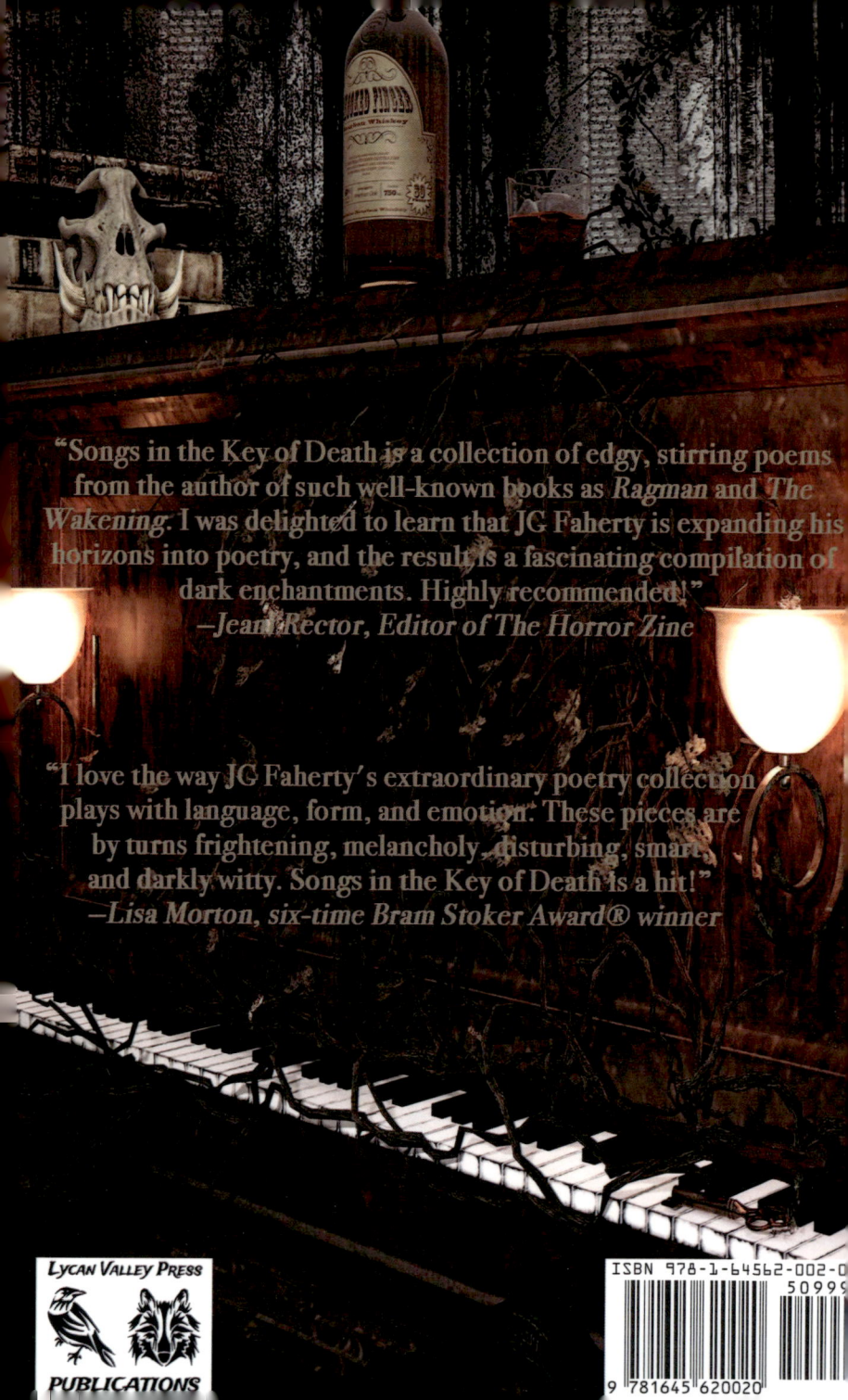

"Songs in the Key of Death is a collection of edgy, stirring poems from the author of such well-known books as *Ragman* and *The Wakening*. I was delighted to learn that JG Faherty is expanding his horizons into poetry, and the result is a fascinating compilation of dark enchantments. Highly recommended!"
—Jean Rector, *Editor of The Horror Zine*

"I love the way JG Faherty's extraordinary poetry collection plays with language, form, and emotion. These pieces are by turns frightening, melancholy, disturbing, smart, and darkly witty. Songs in the Key of Death is a hit!"
—Lisa Morton, *six-time Bram Stoker Award® winner*

LYCAN VALLEY PRESS
PUBLICATIONS

ISBN 978-1-64562-002-0
50999

9 781645 620020